THE LAST TROLL

Steinar Berg

Brian Pilkington

The last troll

FOSSATÚN

Before people settled in Iceland, there were trolls in many parts of Borgarfjörður. They lived in caves and fished in the rivers and lakes. In the rock cliffs from which the district takes its name there was also a flourishing community of elves. After humans arrived, farmed the land and became Christian, the trolls withdrew to the moors and most of the elves retreated inside rocks and hills. One troll woman tried to throw a rock at the church at Hvanneyri when she heard its bells ringing; she missed, but the rock, known as Grásteinn, can still be seen where it landed in the marshland east of the village. Then the troll disappeared inside the mountain Skessuhorn.

Steingrímur and Guðrún began farming together by the river Grímsá. They had been farmhands at Varmilækur, an old farm dating from the settlement, but had managed to buy the land by the riverside, which they called Fossatún. They worked hard to make the farm prosper. They were well liked by the local farmers and were renowned for the caring and respectful way they treated the land. Only one shadow fell on their happiness: they had no children.

Once when Guðrún was picking berries under the bluff at Varmalækjarmúli she looked across the grassy land and said in a half-whisper: "My blessings in life would have been perfect, had the blessing of children not forsaken me." With a sigh she lay down in a grassy hollow by Einbúi, a rock standing up in the slopes there. When she began to doze she seemed to see a man, dressed in fine clothes with a fair complexion, walk out of the rock and say to her: "You have been a good neighbour to my people and myself and made sure that our community has not been disturbed. Now your neighbourliness shall be rewarded and your wish granted." The man seemed to embrace her gently and she was startled from sleep by the earth trembling. Looking up, she saw a rockslide coming down the slope close to where she was lying. It left a cleft in the bluff which has since been called Gunnuklauf, "Guðrún's Cleft."

As winter wore on Guðrún's stomach began to swell and in the spring she gave birth to a bouncing baby boy who was given the name Bergsteinn. Both parents were swarthy, but the baby was strikingly blue-eyed and fair-skinned. He soon grew up to be a handsome and well-built lad, a full head taller than other men.

When Bergsteinn was in his seventeenth year his father called him over and said: "My legs are growing quite weak now and I want to ask you to go on the sheep round-up for me this year and in the future. The shepherds will meet in Reykholt on the autumn equinox, two days from now, and you shall be there."

Bergsteinn's efforts won the admiration of his fellow shepherds, who had never before seen such a big man move so fast over rocks and rough ground. On the final day he was looking for sheep in a dale at the foot of Þórisjökull glacier when a fog suddenly descended and he became separated from the rest of the party. They waited for him for two days, but it was difficult for them to keep the sheep together and the weather was so cold that there were night frosts. So on the third day they returned to their farms, thinking it unlikely that anyone could survive without shelter in the mountains for much longer.

As for Bergsteinn, he reached the side of a lake by evening. He was cold and quite weary by then. There was steam rising at the edge of a block of lava that stood up among the rocks, and the ground was warm. Overcome by fatigue, he lay down in a mossy fissure. Then the rock seemed to open and out stepped a stout man, fairly advanced in years. He was smartly dressed in a blue cowl embroidered with gold, and his hair was white. The man looked at him and spoke in a friendly tone: "Rest now, kinsman, and draw on the energy that is all around." He saw the man walk up to the side of the lake, put his hand under the bank and, faster than the eye could see, he was suddenly holding a beautiful trout, which he gutted and laid out with thyme on a bed of moss over the steam. A short while later the man held the fish up to Bergsteinn's nose, and he leaped to his feet and felt reinvigorated by the delicious aroma. He decided to try to copy what he had seen while he was dozing. It worked for him in exactly the same way. The weather remained unchanged and although he was fairly comfortable on the warm bed of moss and quite well nourished with trout, on the third day he decided to try to find his way back home. After walking for a long time, when the daylight was fading, he thought he could hear singing and followed the sound. Suddenly the fog lifted and he saw that he was only a few feet from the edge of a sheer cliff.

A wondrous sight greeted his eyes: a succession of little waterfalls tumbling down from the edge of the lava and falling in a mighty cascade. He saw a woman kneeling there, doing her washing. As if sensing his presence, she fell silent, stood up and turned to face him. There was a natural bridge of rock over the river that Bergsteinn crossed to her and saw that she was a heavily built woman, with a kind and youthful expression. He greated her, gave a short account of what had happened to him and asked her about herself. She said her name was Drífa. He asked why she was doing the washing. "It is our custom," she answered, "to do the washing for winter when the men have left the moors after rounding up their sheep. My mother has encouraged me to avoid humans, especially latecomers after the round-up." With a faint smile she went on to tell him that she lived with her mother and foster-father in a cave in Hallmundarhraun called Surtshellir, after her maternal grandfather. "Your foster-father, not your father?" Bergsteinn asked. "That's right," she replied. "What happened was that my mother had just reached marrying age when she came upon a shepherd who had lost his way and was exhausted, heading for the glacier, as sometimes happens." She lowered her gaze slightly to conceal a hint of a smile as she told him: "She took him to her cave and put him to bed. To keep him warm she lay down beside him under the blanket. It didn't take him long to warm up and spring

back to life, and they got to know each other rather well."

Soon after the shepherd had left it turned out that the troll girl was with child. Her parents, Surtur and Snjóka, were surprised when her stomach began to swell. Surtur's biggest regret was not being able to eat the visitor. "They decided that Jórunn, my mother, should be given in marriage to the hermit Kleppur, who had never been much of a troll-ladies' man."

Bergsteinn noticed how well-spoken and polite Drífa was. They got on well together, but eventually she made ready to leave and said: "I can see from you, Bergsteinn, that humans need not be the monsters that the trolls often claim they are." He noticed a playful twinkle in her eye, as often before during their conversation. "I've met worse frost giants than you," she said, turning to leave, "and thank you for our talk. But now I must get myself, and the washing, back to the cave." They exchanged polite farewells and headed home. Bergsteinn was given a place to stay for the night in Reykholt and reached Fossatún the following day. His parents were overjoyed to see him, having given him up for dead after the shepherds' news.

For the next eight years, Bergsteinn always became separated from the rest of the party on the last day of the round-up and met Drífa when she came to do her washing by Hraunfossar, the series of waterfalls that pour out of the lava into Hvítá. She always welcomed him by saying: "Shepherds often stray and lose their way." They always parted with great fondness. On the ninth autumn Bergsteinn could tell that Drífa was not as happy as usual and asked her the reason. She said that her mother and foster-father had decided to return to the realm of the trolls, "because the trolls have been moving away for some time. None are left on the Icelandic moors now apart from in Surtshellir." After hesitating for a moment she continued: "My mother and foster-father want to spend the remaining years of their life with their own kind, although they are reluctant to abandon their cave and lands on Hallmundarhraun and Arnarvatnsheiði. They want me to go with them to meet my kin."

Bergsteinn was taken aback at the news and gasped: "My parents are growing old and I am supposed to take over the farm completely next spring. The only fault they find with that is that I have not yet taken a wife. My most memorable times have been with you, Drífa, here by Hraunfossar. So I ask you to become my wife and take over the household at Fossatún. I have been toying with this idea for some time and I believe that, in spite of our different customs and background, we can live happily together. He looked into her eyes and said calmly but emphatically: "Nothing has mattered more to me than the certainty of meeting you here the following year and the yearning to be closer to you has been growing in my heart." After he had spoken these words, he noticed a glint in her eye. She replied: "The same goes for me. I shall discuss it with my dear old mother and my foster-father Kleppur. Come here at the spring equinox if you still feel the same then."

After Drífa went back home, Jórunn and Kleppur noticed that she was unusually quiet. She had long whispered conversations with Gríma the black elf

and they often took long walks. Gríma had always
been Drífa's best friend and she lived up to
her name, which means "Mask". She was
a shape-changer and had gained
knowledge far and wide. Although
she was somewhat older than Drífa
they had formed a close bond.
They spent long stays at their
favourite place, Húsafell, which
always sported beautiful colours
in autumn.

When spring drew near and the cave-dwellers were almost ready to leave, Drífa told her mother and foster-father that she did not intend to go to the realm of the trolls with them, but would stay in the world of men. She told them all about how she had met Bergsteinn and what had passed between them. Her mother Jórunn seemed confused and said: "You should know, Drífa, that when humans began to settle here in Borgarfjörður and occupy the trolls' lands, there were a number of clashes with them. My father Surtur chanced upon Bergsteinn's grandfather, took him away, cooked him in the hot spring at Deildartunguhver and ate him, as was the trolls' custom then." Drífa looked at her mother and said: "Bergsteinn is aware of that, because we have talked much over the washing." Then she added: "The fathers' sins are many, but their children should not be burdened by them. Bergsteinn and I agree on that." Kleppur looked up and said: "A girl in love will always follow her lover," then turned to Jórunn and added: "It is better to work for good than to earn wrath." Jórunn realised they would go their separate ways: "I implore you, Drífa, that if you are not happy, please look for us, no matter how late. And I ask you to accompany your foster-father and me to the gateway to the realm of trolls, which is open to all trolls every evening in the last month of winter." Drífa accompanied them to Skarðsheiði and the peak towering above it, Skessuhorn, which is the gateway to the realm of trolls. There they exchanged farewells before her mother and foster-father vanished inside the mountain.

Bergsteinn was waiting at Hraunfossar when Drífa arrived and their reunion was joyful. He told her of the talk he had had with his parents about his planned marriage and what his mother Guðrún had said. "Bergsteinn dear, there may be problems when different cultures mix, especially when they have been in conflict," she had said. "But you are a man of good appearance and temperament, and I understand that so is your betrothed. Your decision seems carefully considered and there is a hope that you shall grow together by it."

"But you will never have the good fortune to meet my parents," Bergsteinn explained, "because they both died at a short interval around Yuletide. She contracted a fever and my father's sorrow was so great that he followed her."

"So the same goes for our parents, for they have crossed into new worlds and will not be there for us to fall back on," Drífa said, "unless you want to follow me to the realm of the trolls." His look of surprise gave way to a smile when he was gripped tightly by the hand and led off in the direction of Fossatún.

After Bergsteinn and Drífa had settled in they began farming and building a larger house. A man and a woman worked on the farm. Drífa managed them well but they noticed how she would stay indoors until the day drew to a close and the sun started to sink into the sea by Snæfellsjökull glacier in the distance, lighting up the sky behind the Ljósufjöll mountains. When they mentioned this Drífa joked with the people on the farm: "In the realm of trolls the saying goes like this: Make rocks while the sun shines," referring to the way that trolls turn to stone if the rays of the morning sun shine on them. The couple from Fossatún flourished — for they regarded themselves as man and wife, although not officially married. People remarked how skilful Drífa was at weaving and laying fishing nets. She took huge catches of fish from Blundsvatn, a lake belonging to the farm, and cured the trout herself. Her experience far surpassed all that the humans knew and it helped them prosper even more. When Bergsteinn returned from the sheep round-up in the autumn Drífa met him in the yard of the farm. After listening to the story of his travels, she said: "I have news to tell you from Fossatún. The wife is with child and you are as surely the father as I am the mother."

Some of the neighbours made fun of the couple and called Bergsteinn Troll-Boy. But when they saw what a fine match he had made for himself, they soon put an end to all such remarks. All the same, a few local people disapproved that Drífa neither went to church nor had their beautiful daughter baptised – she was simply named Sumarrós.

The priest of Hestþing parish felt uncomfortable that an unchristian woman who was descended from trolls was living in the district, and never visited Fossatún. When Sumarrós was seven years old, the priest bowed to pressure from the local people and decided to visit the farm. Drífa was indoors as usual and Bergsteinn was working outside. She invited the priest in and they began talking. "I understand that Bergsteinn went astray and found you instead," the priest began in an insinuating tone. Drífa glared at him and answered: "He who loses his way finds new paths." "As it happens," the priest replied, changing his tone of voice, "as a young man I got lost in that area and almost met my death. My life was saved by a young troll-woman who carried me back to her cave and nursed me until I could find my way back home. I always intended to reward her for giving me my life but nothing came of it, because it is inappropriate for a novice priest to court trolls."

Surprised by his words, Drífa answered at once: "Few reward the gift of life worthily." She had not wondered about her father's fate and never expected to meet him. Now he was suddenly sitting in front of her. She looked at him firmly and said: "Certainly you left behind a reward. It grew inside the girl who rescued you and later in a cave up on the moors and is now sharing this room with you." The priest turned pale and silent when he heard these words, looked up and saw Drífa in a different light. Clearing his throat, he said: "Then it is more of my business than I thought that your child should not remain ignorant of bliss, but should learn to believe in Christ." Drífa pondered, then decided not to enter into a dispute with the man who gave her life. "We saw far on the moors and we see far from Fossatún," she said, "so I think far-sightedness is most appropriate in this case." After a pause for thought she went on: "Sumarrós will go to Christmas mass with her father, that will help her later to develop the faith she wants to take as her own."

When Christmas drew near, Bergsteinn, Sumarrós and the farmhands from Fossatún got ready to hear evensong on Christmas Eve. After the service they went to a Christmas gathering at Hvanneyri. Father and daughter soon returned to Fossatún while the farmhands stayed to take part in the celebrations. Gríma had visited Drífa at Fossatún as she always did at Yuletide. They had just exchanged farewells in the yard. The weather had been exceptionally warm in the week before Christmas and Drífa was standing outside, expecting the travellers back from the mass. The river was iced over in spite of the fair weather. She soon saw Bergsteinn and Sumarrós walking towards Grímsá. Sumarrós saw her mother in the distance, in the meadow on the other side of the little waterfall called Lækjarfoss, and ran towards her over the ice above it, with Bergsteinn following her. Just before he reached the riverbank there was a cracking noise and the ice split apart under Sumarrós's feet.

Seeing the river forcing its way through, Bergsteinn broke into a run and slid along towards the child. At that moment the ice plunged down from the river and over Lækjarfoss. Bergsteinn managed to grab Sumarrós and lift her up as he sank into the slush and the broken ice. He looked towards Drífa, who had run over and was on the riverbank on the other side in complete horror. Bergsteinn

swung the child and threw her over to her as he shouted: "Catch her now, my love, as you have never caught before." Immediately the surging ice swept him down the gully and under the still-frozen pool at Hörgshylur. Drífa did not take her eyes off her husband, but clutched Sumarrós firmly. She saw him vanish under the ice and she ran along the riverbank with the child in her arms.

Mother and daughter searched for him for most of the moonlit night, until they were tired and cold. They returned to the farm and waited, at a loss for what to do, in the hope that Bergsteinn would find his way home on his own. When that did not happen, Drífa got ready to search for him as soon as the darkness lifted. Eventually she found Bergsteinn's dead body by a waterfall farther downriver; the pool there has been named Viðbjóður – Repulsion – ever since. She took the body and made a grave for her husband on a grassy spot at the top of Stekkjarás, where there is a view over the whole district.

Bergsteinn's death was a great blow to Drífa. She was overcome with anguish, deep sorrow and then fury at herself for having sent her husband to Christmas mass. The farmhands and neighbouring farmers tried to brighten up her life, but to no avail. Realising that this situation could not continue, Sumarrós went out one evening to Búkonulaut, a hollow where she often played games with pebbles, bones from the legs and jaws of sheep, shells and other toys. There she invoked the guardian spirits of the land, as her mother had taught her, and then recited the Lord's Prayer, which she had learnt at the Christmas mass.

The following day Gríma turned up at Fossatún. She went up to Drífa, took her by the hand and led her outside, down to Bergsteinn's grave. "Let us start to rebuild," she said, and began picking up stones and slabs of rock from the ridge. By evening they had piled up a cairn over the grave. Gríma looked at the mound, then at Drífa, and said: "I pronounce that all your discontent shall pass into this rock. Put your right hand on your heart and the left on the uppermost slab. Take a deep breath, close your eyes and think about all the good things that have befallen you on your path through life." Drífa did so and soon felt a warm sensation flowing from her heart and along her left arm, and smoke rose up from the stone. She raised her head and opened her eyes. The overcast sky had cleared, apart from the occasional cloud between her and Snæfellsjökull glacier that reflected the glorious colours of the sunset. Bergsteinn's smiling face etched itself into her mind once more, erasing the death mask that had become embedded there. When she withdrew her hand, its outline was left in the slab of rock. Many people since then have put their hand into the outline and felt the rock's power purge their worries and negative thoughts.

Sumarrós grew up to be an accomplished woman. She maintained a good relationship with her grandfather, the priest, until he died in old age. She was sharp-witted, kind-hearted and resourceful. A gifted craftswoman, she was equally deft with a sewing needle and blacksmith's iron. The neighbours often sought advice from mother and daughter in times of adversity, and they proved helpful to the local people and outsiders alike.

Sumarrós later married a promising man, but they were not blessed with children. Drífa lived with her daughter and son-in-law, but because trolls' years are longer than those of men, she outlived her, and then her childhood friend Gríma moved in to stay with her at Fossatún.